This book belongs to:

_____

W9-BYA-974

Black and White

by MARTY CRISP

illustrated by SHERRY NEIDIGH

rising moon

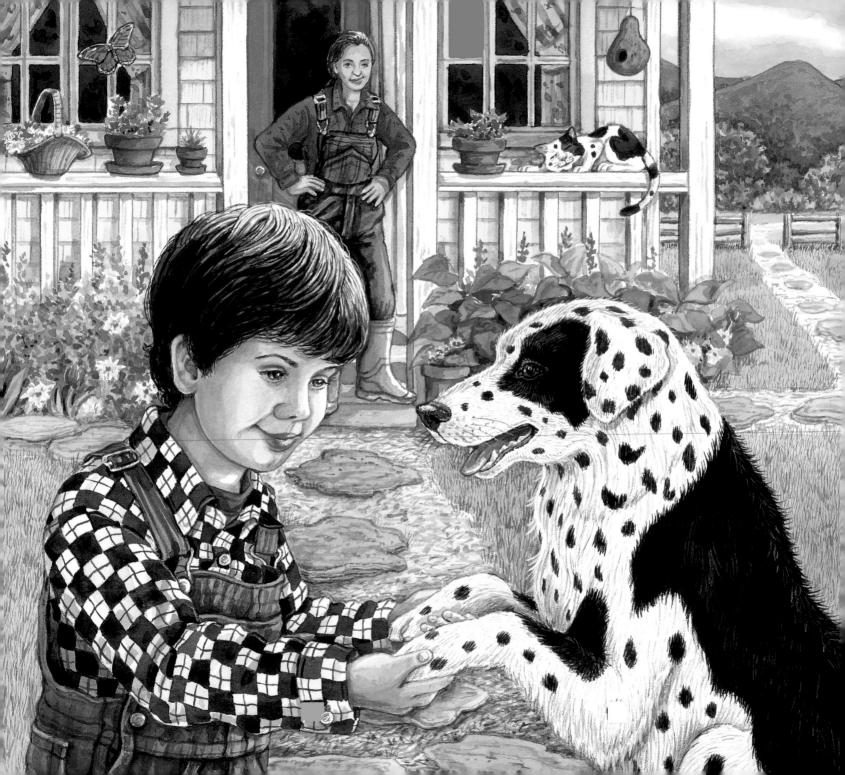

Bud's mother stood on the porch and looked at the new dog.

"Don't name that dog just yet," she said. "If he chases the cows and scares the chickens, he can't be a farm dog. Then we won't be able to keep him."

Bud wanted his new dog to stay. He hoped the pup would fit in with the other farm animals.

"Watch that dog closely now," Bud's mother said, "and we'll see how it goes."

Just then Bud's new dog disappeared around the rabbit hutch!

Bud ran to the edge of the yard to look for his dog. He climbed the fence where the sheep were grazing.

Was that a tail wagging? Sheep don't wag their tails!

Bud looked again, but he didn't see his dog.

Bud ran to the chicken coop to look for his dog.

Was that a floppy ear? Chickens don't have floppy ears!

Bud looked again, but all he saw were chickens clucking and pecking at the ground.

Bud ran to the barn. One llama stamped
her foot.

"Have you seen my dog?" Bud asked the llama.
But the llama just stared at Bud.

"Have you seen my dog?" Bud asked the pigs. But the pigs just grunted and wallowed in the mud.

Bud looked in the goat pen.

Was there an extra goat in the pen today?

Bud looked again, but he didn't see his dog.

Bud ran to the stable. The pony snorted and pricked her ears.

Was there something moving in the shadow of her stall?

Bud looked again, but he didn't see his dog.

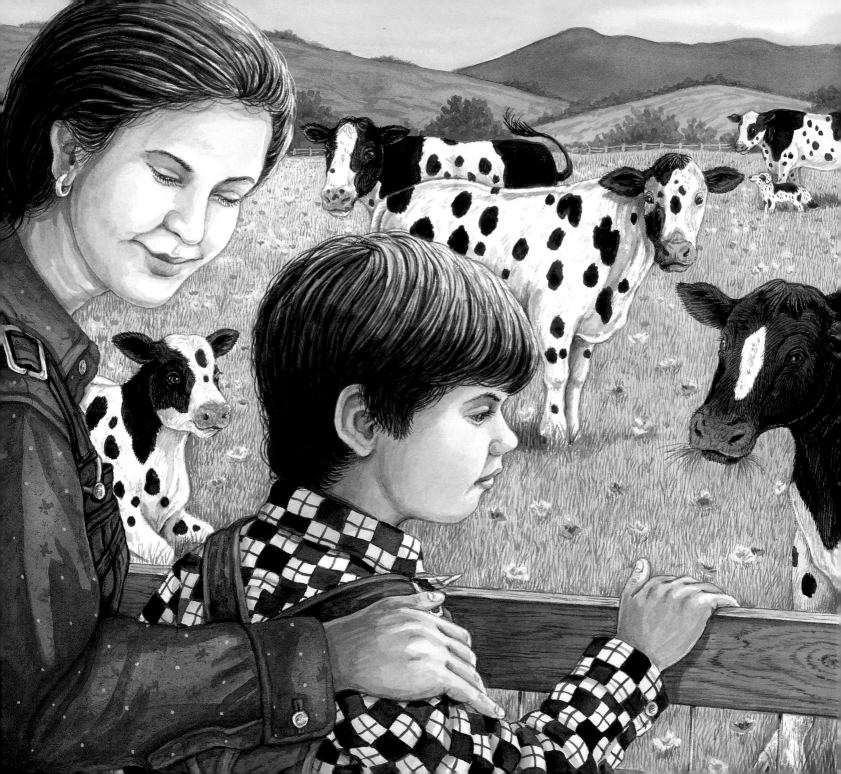

"I can't find my dog anywhere!" Bud cried. He leaned against the fence and watched the cows munch grass in the field.

"Don't worry," Bud's mother told him. "That dog has to be here somewhere."

One cow flicked her tail and bent down.
Her long, pink tongue slurped across something.

"There's my dog!" Bud shouted. "He was here
all along."

"Why, that dog fits in just fine," Bud's
mother said. "It's as plain as black and white."

"That's what I'll name him," Bud said as he bent down to hug his dog. "Black and White—B.W. for short."

B.W. barked just once as if he already knew his name.

MARTY CRISP got the idea for *Black and White* from a true story told to her by a friend. Stopped at a traffic light one day, the friend looked over at a herd of black-and-white cows in a barn paddock and saw one cow bent over as if it were sniffing something on the ground. She couldn't tell what it was until a black-and-white kitten appeared against the cow's pink tongue licking the kitten's head!

Black and White is Marty Crisp's first picture book, though she has published several middle-grade novels—all about dogs. Marty works for the *Lancaster Sunday News* as a staff writer and does freelance writing for a variety of magazines, including *Family Circle, Guideposts,* and *Highlights for Children.* Marty lives in Ephrata, Pennsylvania with her husband, four children, and three dogs.

Photograph by Donna Jernigan

SHERRY NEIDIGH'S first pet was a chicken who accidentally rubbed up against the side of the house while it was being painted green. The chicken ran around half the summer with one green wing. Sherry's parents told her she couldn't have a dog until they had a house with a basement. Finally they did move to a house with a basement, and after a lot of persuasion, Sherry got her first dog—a Dalmatian, which Sherry believed made up for all the lost time she spent without a dog when she was younger.

Sherry has been an artist nearly all her life. She began drawing at the age of two and has been illustrating professionally for the past thirteen years. She has illustrated numerous books, including *Creatures at My Feet,* also from Rising Moon. Sherry lives in Charlotte, North Carolina with a sheltie dog named Basil Knawbone.

For my oldest son, Bud, who always tries harder.

— M. C.

In memory of my mother, Joan Northrup Neidigh, 1929–1998.

— S. N.

The special breeds of animals featured in this book are: Australian shepherd-mix dog, English Spot rabbits, Jacob sheep, Barred Plymouth Rock chickens, llamas, Hampshire pigs, Alpine goats, Appaloosa ponies, and Holstein cows.

The illustrations were rendered in gouache and colored pencil
The text type was set in Vendome
The display type was set in Formata
Composed in the United States of America
Designed by Michael Russell
Edited by Aimee Jackson
Production supervised by Lisa Brownfield
Art directed by Jennifer Schaber

Printed in Hong Kong by Wing King Tong.

www.northlandpub.com

FIRST IMPRESSION
ISBN 0-87358-756-1

Library of Congress Catalog Card Number Pending

115/7.5M/7-00